This igloo book belongs to:

D0546013

....

igl00books

Published in 2019
by Igloo Books Ltd
Cottage Farm
Sywell
NN6 0BJ
www.igloobooks.com

Written by Melanie Joyce
Illustrated by Samantha Meredith

Designed by Jason Shortland
Edited by Hannah Cather

GUA006 0119
2 4 6 8 10 9 7 5 3
ISBN 978-1-78905-653-2

Printed and manufactured in China

10
Little
Friends

igloobooks

Hi, I'm Olly.

I'm all by myself.

Like a teddy on my bed...

... or a book on the shelf.

Knock-Knock!

Here is Sue.

I'm not just **ONE** anymore.

Now, there are **TWO**.

It's fun having friends
to play with me.

Mike comes along.
Then, we are **THREE**.

Ding-dong! goes the doorbell.

Here's one more.

Me, Sue, Mike and Tilly.
That makes **FOUR.**

... and dive.

Josh comes to join in.
Now, there are FIVE.

We build fun dens...

... with pillows and sticks.

"Let me in!" says Ruby.

Then, we are SIX

It's time for a drink and a snack at eleven.

Pete's just in time.
Now, there are SEVEN.

Mummy's scrummy
cupcakes on a plate.

"Yummy!" cries Sophie.
"Now, we are **EIGHT**

Tummies all full,
we lie in a line.

"Surprise!"
cries Billy.

That makes
NINE.

We play together all afternoon and then...

... when Gemma arrives,
it's a perfect **TEN!**